TODAY
Eleanor
WILL BE A

Andrews McMeel
Publishing®

a division of Andrews McMeel Universal

Eleanor

[PASTE PHOTO HERE]

FULL NAME: _____

AGE: _____

Eleanor,

this book is for you!

FROM: _____

MESSAGE: _____

_____

_____

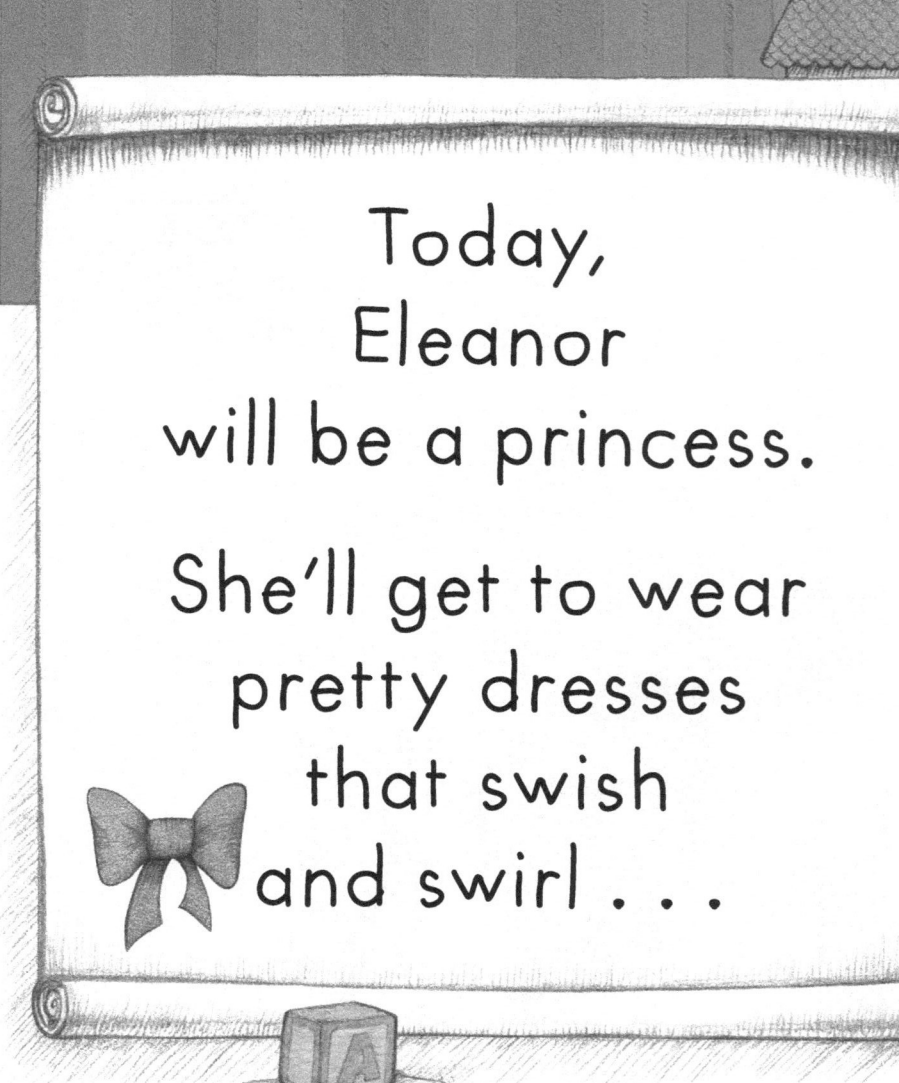

Today,
Eleanor
will be a princess.

She'll get to wear
pretty dresses
that swish
and swirl . . .

and
sparkly shoes
that make her
feel fancy.

Eleanor
will ride in
a royal carriage
wherever
she goes . . .

and wear
the most
beautiful
crown covered
with jewels.

But, mommy
says princesses
don't get
to play in
the mud.

Maybe
Eleanor
will be
a princess
tomorrow . . .

PRINCESS
Eleanor's
FAVORITE THINGS

COLOR: _____

FOOD: _____

GAME: _____

ANIMAL: _____

SONG: _____

MOVIE: _____

DRAW
PRINCESS
Eleanor

Andrews McMeel Publishing
a division of Andrews McMeel Universal
1130 Walnut Street, Kansas City, Missouri 64106

www.andrewsmcmeel.com

Library of Congress Control Number: 2014946447

Written by Paula Croyle
Illustrated by Heather Brown

CPSIA information can be obtained
at www.ICGtesting.com
Printed in the USA
LVHW06*0206240518
578347LV00017B/108/P